JLK

RH

Also by Elizabeth Starr Hill

*Bird Boy*

*Chang and the Bamboo Flute*

# WILDFIRE!

# WILDFIRE!

ELIZABETH STARR HILL

Pictures by ROB SHEPPERSON

Farrar, Straus and Giroux / New York

www.fsgkidsbooks.com

Library of Congress Cataloging-in-Publication Data
Hill, Elizabeth Starr.
    Wildfire! / Elizabeth Starr Hill ; pictures by Rob Shepperson.—1st ed.
        p.  cm.
    Summary: Living with his great grandmother in rural Florida, ten-year-old
Ben looks forward to the Fourth of July celebrations, but the day becomes
complicated by the presence of a new neighbor boy, a stray puppy, and local
wildfires.
    ISBN 0-374-31712-7
    [1. Self-perception—Fiction.   2. Country life—Fiction.   3. Orphans—
Fiction.   4. Fourth of July—Fiction.   5. Forest fires—Fiction.   6. Florida—
Fiction.]   I. Shepperson, Rob, ill.   II. Title.

PZ7.H55Whf2004
[Fic]—dc22
                                                              2003049314

*To my good friend Ruth Stewart, with thanks*
—E.S.H.

# WILDFIRE!

# 1

Ben took one more biscuit, slathered it with Goomby's wild-orange marmalade, and stuffed it into his mouth. His grandparents had already finished breakfast. Goomby, his great-grandmother, had eaten just a few quick bites, and was through. Smiling, she asked Ben, "Want more?"

He shook his head. They put all the dishes in the sink and joined Grandpa in the living room.

Grandpa was watching the TV news. The pictures on the screen were scary. They showed orange and red flames crackling through trees, torching giant pines as though they were tooth-

picks. The weather had been very hot and dry for weeks. Wildfires were burning all over Florida. New ones blazed up every day.

"These are south of here, but they're in our forest," Grandpa said.

"How far?" Goomby asked.

"Down around Worthington," Grandpa answered his mother. "Far enough to be safe."

"This time. For now," Goomby answered.

"Yes. For now." Grandpa's voice was strong and reassuring, but his lean tanned face showed his worry. They all knew how sparks could travel in the air, starting a new fire someplace else.

Their little village of Bending Creek had no fire department of its own. There had not been a bad fire here for years, but if there were, they would have to depend on firefighters coming from Carville, the nearest big town. That was thirty miles away.

"More coffee?" Goomby asked her son. Grandma had already gone to her waitress job at the Happy Day Café.

"No, gotta get to work. Full crew coming in today." He ruffled Ben's hair. "Be good, you two."

Goomby grinned. "Maybe. Maybe not."

Grandpa laughed. He picked up the lunch she had packed for him and left for his job at the sawmill.

Goomby turned off the TV and bustled away to wash the breakfast dishes. Ben joined her in the kitchen.

Out the window, the familiar woods looked strange and a little frightening. Even though the fires were far away, the smoke had spread here, gathering in tall pines and oaks and vines and scrub palmettos, blurring all the forest greens.

"How about doing an errand for me in town?" Goomby asked Ben. "I need a couple more things for tomorrow."

Tomorrow was the Fourth of July. Goomby always prepared a lot of food for the holiday.

Ben was glad to help her. His parents had been killed in a car crash six years ago, when he was four years old.

Ben and his parents had lived in another town

then. He hadn't known his grandparents and Goomby very well.

He had a confused memory of relatives coming to the house, trying to decide what would happen to him. Then Goomby had said, "Ben belongs to us. He's coming home with us."

Others in the family had argued that this might make too much work for her. But she always answered, "I'm sixty-eight, not a hundred and ten. And *he's our boy*."

Ben never forgot that. "He's our boy." His sorrow and fear had begun to lift in that moment.

Grandma and Grandpa had agreed, of course. But in Ben's heart it had really been Goomby's decision. She had given him this home and this life.

He told her, "I'll do your errands right now, if you want."

"Oh, good." She gave him some money and a list.

Cornmeal, beans, molasses, red cabbage and white cabbage for two-color coleslaw, one ripe avocado. Ben knew he could get all this in Mr. Meehan's grocery store. Goomby also wanted two tiny lamps for a dollhouse she was making for a church sale. He would have to go to Cindy's Craft Shop for those.

"Okay." He went off, whistling.

He passed the American flag Grandpa had put on the porch in honor of the Fourth of July. There were flags on all the neighbors' porches, too. They made patches of bright color on the little houses along the dusty road.

Ben loved the Fourth. Tomorrow there would be an all-day celebration in Bending Creek Park —a parade, then the picnic, then games and contests and a speech by Mayor Jolson. It was the same speech every year, about how this was a day to remember, the day America became a free country. Then a band concert and more eating.

Usually the day ended with fireworks over the lake. Grandpa had bought a box a month ago so he and Ben could set off some just for fun, before the official display. But fireworks were banned this year because of the fire danger. Still, there would be plenty of other things to do.

At the grocery, Mr. Meehan weighed out cornmeal and beans. He chose a perfect avocado. He wedged in a jar of molasses. With the two cabbages, the food almost filled up a big brown paper bag.

"Got room in there for a few caramels?" he asked Ben.

"Sure do!" Ben said eagerly. Mr. Meehan threw them in without charge.

Ben thanked him and left the grocery. He turned onto a side road for Cindy's Craft Shop, happy about the caramels.

As he came around the corner, he saw Elliot Lorton outside Cindy's. Elliot called to him, "Hi, Ben! How you folks doing, off there in the backwoods?" He sounded friendly, but Ben heard an edge of scorn in his voice.

Ben's spirits sank. Elliot and his parents had recently moved to Bending Creek from a northern city. Elliot seemed to think his city ways made him better than the people of Bending Creek—

and especially better than Ben, who was, as Elliot kept reminding him, only a boy living on a dirt road in the backwoods.

Ben hurried into Cindy's shop without responding and tried to slam the door shut, but Elliot followed right behind him.

Now, Ben realized, he would have to buy two tiny lamps. That made him feel foolish. He hoped Elliot wouldn't notice what he was buying.

"Why, hello, Ben," Cindy said cordially from behind the counter. She had a loud voice. "Looking for something for the dollhouse?"

# 2

Ben's cheeks flushed. He mumbled, "Lamps."

Cindy brought some out from the rear of the store. Elliot grinned, but he didn't say anything.

Ben muttered an explanation about Goomby's project. "I'll take those two." He thrust the money at Cindy, longing to get out of there. She put the lamps in a little box and gave him his change. He stuffed it all in with the groceries and bolted from the shop.

Elliot came with him. "You and your folks going to move into a dollhouse?" He chuckled. "Not much of a change for you, I guess."

Elliot never missed a chance to remind Ben that their home was only a wooden bungalow in a clearing in the woods, while the Lortons—Elliot and his mother and father—lived in a nice big house in town.

Ben didn't answer this. He said, "Well, so long," and sprinted around the corner.

But Elliot was right there with him. "What's the rush? It's too hot to hurry."

It was. The withering heat, laced with smoke from the fires, made the air feel hard to breathe, and carrying the big grocery bag didn't help. Ben slowed down. They trudged along silently, kicking up dust from the dry dirt road.

As they neared Ben's bungalow, Elliot asked, "Do animals live in the woods?"

"Sure. Millions of 'em."

Elliot glanced at the trees beside the road. "You see them much?"

A squirrel chittered in a pine. An armadillo rustled through some fallen palm fronds, right beside the road. Ben said, "There's a couple right there."

"I meant bigger animals."

"We see deer a lot, mostly when it's getting dark. Foxes sometimes. There's bears and bobcats too, but they don't come out as much. And where the creek goes through the trees, there's alligators, and—"

"Snakes?" Elliot broke in.

"Well, yeah. Sure."

Elliot shied away from the woods. "What a place to live," he said in disgust. Then he added amiably, "No offense."

Ben gritted his teeth. This was *his* place to live, and he liked it. And he didn't like Elliot for trying to make him ashamed of it.

They reached his house. Elliot said, "Air-conditioning would feel good right now. But I guess you don't have that."

"Yes, we do," Ben answered stiffly. "You can come in, if you want."

Elliot followed him.

It was cool in the bungalow. Their air conditioners were noisy window units, but they worked fine.

Goomby said hello to Elliot. He answered quickly and politely, "Morning, ma'am. Another hot day."

Goomby nodded. She thanked Ben for the groceries and the change and put them away. "These must be for you." She gave him the caramels. Ben stuffed them in his pocket for later.

She opened the box with the little lamps in it. Ben hoped any talk about them would be brief.

"They're perfect," Goomby said. "How about some lemonade? You boys thirsty?"

"Yes!" Ben said.

"That would be great." Elliot smiled.

They sat at the kitchen table. Goomby poured out two big glasses. While they drank the sweet cold lemonade, she put a ham on to boil. They would have it sliced cold at the picnic tomorrow. She rolled chicken pieces in cornmeal and placed them in the big skillet to fry. The kitchen began to smell delicious.

Ben and Elliot seemed to have nothing more to say to each other, and Ben wished the other boy

would leave. But Elliot looked as if he were set-
tling down for a while. He hummed, sipped the
last of his drink, tapped his fingers on the table.
He looked bored. Elliot often looked that way, as
if there were better things to do—anywhere but
here.

"Want to play checkers?" Ben asked finally. He
was getting bored himself, just sitting here.

Elliot shrugged. "I guess so."

They played three games. Elliot lost all three.
Ben was pretty good at checkers, but Elliot said he
was used to playing with much better players and
that Ben's blunders had thrown him off his game.

Ben snorted and replied, "Oh, yeah? Last year I
beat three champions over in Carville. There was
a contest and they'd already played some other
guys, and these were the winners, and I beat 'em
all."

This wasn't quite true—he had actually beaten
one of them and lost to the other two—but today
Elliot had lost fair and square, and Ben hated his
attitude. He tossed the pieces in the box and

folded the board, saying, "That's enough checkers."

At last Elliot got up to leave. Then Miss Alice, their neighbor up the road, rang her I've-got-news bell, and Goomby said, "Oh, dear, I wonder what Alice wants to tell us. I hope it's nothing bad."

Elliot rolled his eyes. One of the many things he thought was funny about Bending Creek was the way people rang bells to say things, but Ben knew it was a good system, here in the country. Mr. Hendrick, who lived on the other side of Miss Alice, always used a brass bell to call his cats in at night. Goomby rang her noisy old come-home bell to call the family in to supper. And Miss Alice gathered the neighbors this way when she had something special to say.

Ben liked the bells. They were like voices to him, the voices of Bending Creek—his family, his neighbors, his friends.

Goomby turned off the burner under the ham. She finished frying the chicken and put the pieces onto paper toweling to drain and cool. She turned off that burner, too, and double-checked to be sure she hadn't left anything on. The threat of fire made everyone extra careful.

Then she whisked off her apron and they all went next door to hear Miss Alice's news.

3

Miss Alice was on her porch when they got there. She was holding a skinny little white puppy in her arms. The pup looked at Goomby and Ben and Elliot with scared dark eyes. Hesitantly, it wagged its tail.

"Why, where did he come from?" Goomby exclaimed. She reached out a wrinkled tanned hand and stroked the pup. "He's not from around here."

Mr. Hendrick came over from next door. The Olsen family, who lived farther up the road, hurried to join them. The neighbors agreed. Nobody had ever seen the pup before.

"I think he was dropped off by a car this morning," Miss Alice told them. "I saw a car come through, not anybody we know. And then there was this poor little mite, out in the road."

Mr. Olsen made a sound of disgust. "It's terrible how people do that with a pet sometimes. They don't want them anymore, so they drop them off like a sack of peanuts."

"That's awful," Elliot said indignantly. "Hello, boy. Hello." He stroked the puppy's nose.

"I can't keep him," Miss Alice said. "I'm at my sister's so much. I hoped one of you might take him."

Mrs. Olsen shook her head. "We've got three dogs already."

"I'm more of a cat person," Mr. Hendrick said.

Ben looked into the pup's frightened eyes. He imagined how awful it would be, to be dumped in a strange place with strange people. He had a dim memory of feeling like that when his parents died.

He longed to say, "I'll take him."

He had never had a dog. But when summer was over, he would be in school all day. Grandma and Grandpa would be working, as usual. It would mean extra trouble for Goomby.

He felt Goomby's sharp dark eyes on his face. She drew a breath, and Ben felt a flare of hope. But before she could speak, Elliot said, "I'd love to have a dog."

Miss Alice turned to him gratefully. "Really, Elliot?"

"Yes, ma'am. It sounds like fun."

"Well, it's a big responsibility, too," Miss Alice told him. "I'd have to ask your mother."

"Okay. I guess you don't have a phone?"

"Yes, I do," she replied. She hesitated for a moment, studying Elliot's face. He wore a sincere, hopeful expression, with none of his usual superior smirk.

Ben's thoughts flashed to all the times Elliot had made fun of Miss Alice and her bells, always behind her back, of course. And now Miss Alice was looking at him with a kind of fondness! Grownups never seemed to see through Elliot, he was so polite, so two-faced. Ben felt a familiar despair. He wished he could be like that, saying and doing the right things to get his own way. But he never knew what to say.

He didn't know now.

Miss Alice made up her mind. She asked Elliot, "What's your number?"

He told her. She went off, still holding the puppy.

The boys waited silently while she made the call. Ben's heart thumped. He thought Mrs. Lorton might say no, and then Goomby might say . . .

But in a minute Miss Alice was back, smiling. "It's fine with your mother. You can take him right now, if you want."

"Oh, I do."

She placed the pup in his arms. "You can buy a collar and leash at Nelson's Hardware. You'll need to hold on to him until he learns his name and where he lives."

Elliot nodded. "This is wonderful, Miss Alice. Thanks a lot."

"Well, you're welcome. Give him a good home," she answered, beaming.

Elliot put the pup down. The little dog looked bewildered. Elliot snapped his fingers and said, "Come on, fella."

The pup spotted a squirrel. He ran toward it, barked, and scared it up a tree.

Elliot laughed. He repeated, "Come *on*."

Miss Alice said, "I should have given him a rope to tie on that pup."

The pup threw one more bark up the tree at the squirrel, then trotted after Elliot.

Ben watched them go. There was an ache inside him.


After supper Grandma and Grandpa and Goomby watched TV. Ben sat alone out on the porch. The woods grew dark. Fireflies appeared dimly, their lights blurred by smoke.

Ben imagined what it would be like if the pup were his. Ideas bubbled in him, sweet as soda.

He imagined the dog waiting for him to come home from school, sitting on the porch. The pup would see him walking along the road. He would run forward, wagging his tail really hard. Maybe he would jump up and lick Ben's face. Ben had seen one of the Olsen dogs do that, almost knocking the littlest Olsen kid off his feet. The memory of it made him laugh.

He would teach the puppy to catch a Frisbee, and not to chase cats. Mr. Hendrick hated it when a dog chased his cats.

They would go fishing together, keeping each other company on the bank of the creek. A wonderful sense of hospitality warmed Ben, thinking about it. He would show the puppy his favorite places, share a piece of corn pone with him, maybe teach him to swim.

But after a while, sitting in the dark, his imaginings faded and he was just Ben again, alone. It was Elliot who had the dog.

# 4

Ben and his family got up early the next morning to pack Goomby's food hampers in the truck, along with a water jug and blankets. The box of fireworks and matches were still in the pickup— Grandpa had stored them there before the ban— but they didn't take up much space. Ben stepped around them to fit in one last hamper.

He smelled honey cake. He couldn't resist lifting the hamper's lid and sneaking a piece into his mouth. It melted on his tongue, all buttery sweetness.

Goomby came up behind him and rapped his hand lightly. "No more!"

"Okay. It's really good, Goomby." Ben licked the crumbs off his fingers and set to work again.

After the food was all loaded, they drove the short distance to the park. When they got there, Goomby and Grandma chose a place for them to spread their blankets, under a huge live oak tree. This would give them shade for most of the day.

"Going to be another scorcher," Grandpa said, wiping his brow.

The day was hazy and very hot. Across the road in the forest, smoke hung heavily in the still air.

Several other families brought their blankets and food to the shelter of the oak. Elliot and his parents came with the puppy. The little dog was panting in the heat.

"May we join you?" Mrs. Lorton asked.

"Why sure." Grandma smiled.

"You bet," Grandpa added. "Sit right down."

"We're not used to weather like this," Mr. Lorton said.

"Well, Florida summers are fierce till you get used to them," Grandma said.

"I don't think I ever will." Mrs. Lorton sighed.

The pup tried to climb into Ben's lap. He still wasn't wearing a collar or leash. Elliot grabbed him by the scruff of the neck and yanked him back.

"What're you going to name him?" Ben asked.

Elliot shrugged. "Dunno." His first interest in the pup seemed to be wearing off.

Mrs. Lorton asked, "You're Ben, aren't you?"

"Yes, ma'am."

She smiled. "Isn't it nice that Elliot has a dog now? He's never had one before."

She made it sound as though the whole world should rejoice.

"Yes, ma'am," Ben said.

"I've told the boy he'll have to take good care of him," Mr. Lorton said. "That teaches a kid responsibility," he added to Goomby.

"Mmm," Goomby responded.

"I wonder if we should have brought a water bowl for him," Mrs. Lorton asked.

"I should think so," Goomby answered. "Take this." She handed Mrs. Lorton a bowl.

"Oh, thank you." Mrs. Lorton took it and filled it with water from her thermos. The pup lapped thirstily. When the water was gone, he looked up hopefully, as if asking for more.

Elliot was gazing off to where the parade was forming. He paid no attention to the pup.

More and more people gathered. Many were waving little flags.

Soon the band struck up "The Star-Spangled Banner." Everyone scrambled to their feet. The parade began.

Bending Creek's Yankee Doodle Dandies, the marching band, led the way. They were followed by stars from Miss Louise's dance classes, who pranced forward, twirling batons. They threw the batons in the air and spun them, caught them, then tossed them up and caught them again, never dropping one.

"I don't know how they do that," Grandma murmured.

A slow-moving open car appeared, carrying

Mayor Jolson. He was standing, flourishing a big straw hat. People cheered and applauded.

Then two police cars passed, sirens blaring, cops waving, and everybody cheered again.

Next came decorated vehicles advertising local businesses. Mr. Meehan from the grocery was driving a truckload of brightly colored fake vegetables and giant jars of food. Mr. Meehan was popular in town. The crowd laughed. Somebody called out jokingly, "Hey, Meehan, you gonna have a special on those tomatoes?"

Cindy, the craft shop lady, had glued balls of knitting yarn and sequins onto a banner and wrapped it around her car. Mr. Cass, who owned the bowling alley, was dressed as a clown. He walked along juggling pins while an assistant rolled a huge make-believe bowling ball behind him.

Last, and best, was a float bearing Bunny Johnson, Miss Bending Creek. She wore a pink dress and a rhinestone crown. The float was decorated with hundreds of paper roses, and Bunny, perspiring but smiling gamely, waved and waved.

At the end, the Yankee Doodle Dandies appeared again and played the parade off, to more cheers and applause.

People settled back down on their blankets.

"Wasn't that something?" Grandma said proudly to the Lortons.

"Our best parade ever!" Goomby agreed.

Mr. and Mrs. Lorton murmured something polite. But looking at the ground, Elliot muttered, "You've got to be kidding."

Ben felt a stab of anger and shame. He wished Elliot would go away, but no such luck.

Mayor Jolson climbed to the bandstand. He made his usual speech about freedom and how this was a day to remember.

Ben could tell from Elliot's face that he thought the speech was dumb and boring, just like the parade. Just like everything else in Bending Creek. And this year there wouldn't even be fireworks.

Ben had looked forward to this day so much, but now he saw it as Elliot did, and it seemed empty and flat. He wished there were something more to look forward to today, something unexpected and exciting.

Mr. Olsen, who was the scoutmaster, organized games for the kids, but they were the same old games. There was a tug-of-war, a ringtoss, a lot of pickup games of catch. Ben and Al Mason were partners in the three-legged race. They won. Elliot won the ringtoss. In the tug-of-war he and Ben were on the same side. It seemed to Ben that he pulled a lot harder than Elliot, but he wasn't sure Elliot noticed.

Ben played until he was tired, but he still wanted something else to happen. Something different.

He sat with some of the other kids on the ground under an orchid tree. The tree had been pretty earlier in the summer, covered with deep pink flowers. Now it was sun-dried and sorry-looking, like everything else.

"Usually we have fireworks after dark," Lucy Johnson was telling Elliot.

"My kid brother brought a lot of sparklers last year," Jimmy Kyler said.

"I set off a lot of stuff with my grandpa," Ben said. He added, "We would have done that this year, too. We already bought them."

"What did you do with them?" Elliot asked.

"We still have them over in the truck," Ben said.

Elliot's eyes got interested. "Right here, you mean?"

Suddenly Ben felt uneasy. "Yeah," he said. "But we can't set them off this year. You know that."

"Sure, I know that," Elliot said with his superior smirk. "But how about firing just a *few* of them? Who'd ever know?"

"Oh, do it, Ben!" Lucy chimed in excitedly. She was an older girl, always a ringleader in any kind of trouble. "We *oughta* have fireworks!"

A restless little itch scratched inside Ben. He thought of rockets exploding, of all the real fun of the Fourth of July. Finally, this day would become special!

He hesitated. "We might get in a lot of trouble," he said.

"We could take them down to the lake," Lucy put in. "Nobody'd see us from here!"

"Somebody might," Jimmy Kyler offered timidly.

"You're always such a chicken," Lucy told the little boy scornfully.

"I *dare* you," Elliot told Ben. "Bet you don't have the nerve."

Ben's face reddened. "Sure I do. It's just—" he stammered.

"Just what?" Lucy demanded.

"*Double* dare you!" Elliot taunted.

"Okay! Okay! I was thinking of doing it anyway," Ben lied. A thrilled, reckless feeling took hold of him. "Meet me at the lake right after the band concert."

"Oh, gee," Jimmy Kyler said apprehensively.

"Are you in or out?" Lucy asked him relentlessly.

Jimmy was not a ringleader of anything, but he usually followed any suggestion. "In," he quavered.

Four or five other kids were gathered around

them. "Don't say anything to anybody else," Ben
cautioned. They all shook their heads.

"Okay. See you there then."

They nodded numbly.

Giddy with power, Ben told Elliot, "That
means you, too."

"Right." Elliot grinned. "Let's get something
to eat."

# 5

Together Ben and Elliot returned to their families. Ben flung himself down on the blanket near Goomby. She had spread out jugs of lemonade and sodas and more food. All over the park, people began eating and drinking again.

Mrs. Lorton had been holding the pup. Now she handed him back to Elliot. "I think he's hungry."

Elliot nodded absently. He gave the pup some meat loaf.

The band concert began. The sky was turning rosy gold with sunset. The music was tuneful and familiar. People hummed the old songs. It was a peaceful time of day, but not for Ben. He felt more and more nervous.

The Yankee Doodle Dandies started "The Stars and Stripes Forever." This was always the last number in the concert.

Ben jumped up and murmured to Goomby, "Be back soon." She nodded, and he sprinted away, carrying an empty Coke bottle with him. He could feel Elliot watching him, waiting for the concert to end.

At the truck, he looked back to be sure nobody could see him. The parking lot was a fair distance from the picnic area, with trees and bushes in between. The sun was setting, and smoke dulled the air. Anyway, nobody was near enough to catch a clear view of him.

He heard applause at the finish of the concert. Ben knew most people would stay for a while, enjoying the last of the day. Someone began strumming a guitar.

He got the box of fireworks and some matches from the pickup. The box was pretty big, but not too heavy. Still holding the empty Coke bottle, Ben balanced the box against his chest and lugged it to the path leading to the lake, at the far end of the park.

The tall trees of the forest loomed around the lake. Many of their needles had turned brown in the drought. Ben took the box to the rock where he and Grandpa had set off fireworks the year before—when there had been plenty of rain and no worries about fire.

Ben glanced at the tinder-dry forest, then put his own worries and hesitation out of his mind. Lucy and Jimmy and the others were running along the path toward him, with Elliot close behind. The pup was running loose around Elliot's ankles.

"Welcome to the Fourth of July show!" Ben called. He wrenched the top off the box and took out a rocket. Then, aware again of the nearness of the pines, he hesitated.

"Let's get started," Lucy said.

"It's not dark yet," Jimmy Kyler objected. "Anyway, I don't think we should be doing this."

"*Come on*, before everybody chickens out," Lucy urged Ben.

Elliot strolled up. "Maybe Ben's the chicken." He smiled coolly.

"Who, me?" Quickly Ben took out a rocket. "This is it! Get ready!" He stuck the rocket's long balsa-wood tail into the Coke bottle and set the bottle in the sand. Now the rocket's black nose was pointed to the sky, slightly over the lake.

Ben's hands were sweating. They shook a little as he lit a match and ignited the fuse in the tail. He shouted, "Stay back, everybody!"

They all knew it was dangerous to get near the rocket once that fuse was lit. The puppy barked, confused, following first one person, then another. The fuse burned up to the rocket's red body, the part that was filled with explosives. When it reached it, the rocket shot into the air in a high arc. It made a shattering noise and burst into a shower of colored floating sparks. They drifted toward the water, and toward the towering pines.

The puppy yelped in terror and rushed away, running for shelter in the forest.

Ben yelled, "Come back!" But the dog was gone, out of sight.

Elliot said, "Hey! That was great!" He moved toward the box. "How about some more, Ben?"

Suddenly the fun was over for Ben. He could hear the puppy, yelping still. He slammed the box shut and said to Elliot, "You better get your dog! He went into the woods!"

"Oh." Elliot looked around, then groaned. "How am I supposed to find him in there?"

Ben didn't answer. He plunged in among the trees. "Here, boy," he called. He wished the dog had a name. "Come back, fella!"

Behind him, one of the kids said, "I need to get back to my folks."

"Me, too," Lucy Johnson decided.

They began to disperse.

"Hey, Ben, wait for me!" Elliot called. He blundered toward Ben through the pines as the terrified little dog scampered ahead.

# 6

"Do you know where we're going?" Elliot gasped after a few minutes.

"No," Ben admitted. He had never been in this part of the forest before. He seldom roamed in the woods, even near his own house. Much of the ground was rough, littered with fallen sticks and branches from past hurricanes, and overgrown with vines and scrub palmettos.

They could hear the headlong flight of the puppy ahead. Finally they glimpsed him and trailed him deeper into the woods.

Sunset faded from the sky. A weird misty dusk

blanketed the forest. The boys ran on and on, first this way, then that. At every twist and turn they could see the pale form of the puppy, scrambling, small and desperate, far ahead of them.

"It'll be dark soon." Ben heard the fear in Elliot's voice.

"I know that."

After a while the puppy slowed down. For a few moments Ben thought they were gaining on him. Then the dog spotted an armadillo and dashed sidewise after it, barking. With surprising speed, the armadillo raced off through the fallen palm fronds. The puppy, following in this new direction, went after it.

Ben and Elliot groaned. The pup was farther away from them than ever. But he couldn't reach the armadillo. At last he faltered and gave up.

"Good boy! Come here!" Ben called. He clapped his hands.

The pup looked in his direction.

"That's it! Come on!" Ben called.

Exasperated, Elliot echoed, "Here! *Now*, you dumb dog!"

The pup took several steps toward them. Then his attention seemed to be diverted. He looked away. After a minute Ben saw what the dog saw. About forty feet away, a group of wild pigs were rooting in a clearing. The last light of day shone down through the break in the trees and illumined them plainly.

Ben had always known that huge pigs lived in the woods, but he had seen them only a few times. They moved around mostly at night, hunting for food. They were about three feet tall at the shoulder and large-bodied, with dark bristly hair and sharp tusks. The boars—the males—guarded the group, and Ben knew they could be ferocious, especially when protecting their young.

And among the other pigs were two young piglets.

Curious, the pup moved nearer the group. One boar separated from the others and grunted warningly. It trotted a few steps toward the puppy. Obviously this boar was ready to defend the whole group against danger. It was the largest of them all, its tusks glimmering like curved knives.

The dog barked, sounding a little scared now.

"Oh, no," Elliot moaned under his breath.

The pig grunted again and trotted nearer.

This sent the pup into a frenzy of barking. He made a short rush at the boar. He stopped before getting too near. But the pig came after him, snorting and grunting angrily.

At last the pup got scared enough to turn and head for Ben, away from the boar. The boar kept coming. The pup was right in his path, and in front of the pup were Elliot and Ben.

Elliot panicked. He ran, stumbling in the near-dark, getting away.

Ben stood his ground, badly frightened. Then he raced toward the pup. The enraged boar was getting closer by the moment.

Before the furious pig could reach them, Ben managed an extra burst of speed and scooped up the quivering puppy. Holding the dog in his arms, he reversed direction, trying to choose a way that offered the best chance of escape.

Outside the clearing, dusk was darkening to night. It was hard to see much of anything. Ben

knew the best thing he could do would be to climb a tree, but none of those around him had low-enough branches to give him a foothold. And climbing with the puppy in his arms would be almost impossible anyhow.

The pig snorted. It was only a few yards away now. And Ben knew that it was capable of tearing them both to pieces.

# 7

He had to take cover. Desperately Ben scanned the small visible space around him. He could make out a clump of scrub palmetto nearby, its stunted clusters of short trunks and fronds forming dense bunches of foliage. Holding tight to the puppy, Ben dived into it and burrowed until he and the pup were out of sight.

His heart pounded. He felt as if his chest might burst.

The pup whimpered softly, then quieted.

Ben waited. The boar was right outside the palmettos. He heard its harsh, angry breathing. But it did not charge the dense foliage.

Ben waited. He knew the boar was still there, and he didn't dare move.

Then there were new sounds. It was as though a strange mood was overtaking the forest. The woodland creatures were stirring. Ben heard a wide rustle of squirrels and armadillos through the underbrush, and a quiet but hasty slither of snakes.

He peeked out between palmetto fronds. The boar was not far from him, but its gaze was set in another direction.

Ben looked that way. A glow had appeared in the woods. The boar snuffled, lifted its head, and sniffed the air.

Ben smelled it, too. It was a faint new wave of smoke.

A river of fright seemed to rush through his stomach. The glow brightened against the sky. Then flickers of orange and red light showed through the trees.

Ben recognized them with horror. *Flames.* There was a new fire in the forest.

He remembered sparks from the exploded rocket drifting over the trees. This was just what people had feared might happen, what the whole town had been warned about—the reason fireworks had been banned.

The boar snorted and tossed its head. It trotted back to its group and began rounding them up.

A deer crashed through the woods, escaping from the fire. The puppy trembled and tried to hide his head against Ben's chest.

Holding him, Ben clambered out of the palmettos. He sensed the alarm of all the forest creatures. Darting lizards raced up trees, then down again, then off to fallen logs. A great horned owl hooted overhead and flapped away.

"Ben!" Elliot's frantic voice called from somewhere. "Help me!"

"Where are you?" Ben shouted. "I can't see you."

"I don't know where I am," Elliot answered in a despairing wail. "Help me! I hurt my leg!"

They exchanged a few more shouts. Finally Ben found Elliot lying on the ground beside a fallen log. "What happened?" he asked.

"I jumped over the log and landed on that thing." Elliot gestured to a low spiny yucca called Spanish bayonet. Its long, rigid leaves were as sharp as swords. "Cut me up so bad—" Elliot extended his leg so Ben could see it.

The leg was gashed in several places and trickling blood.

Ben had run into Spanish bayonet himself a few times. He knew how painful the stabs were, but they were not deep.

"The bleeding'll stop pretty soon." Ben clutched the puppy against his chest with one hand and extended the other to Elliot. The drift of smoke made him cough. "Here, get up."

He thought Elliot would be pleased to see the pup safe, but he didn't seem to care. "The woods are on fire, aren't they?" Elliot's voice was a thin thread of fear.

"Yes. We've got to move. It's coming this way."

"How do you know?" Elliot asked. He looked terrified.

"The animals know. *Get up*." He pulled Elliot upright.

As Elliot saw the flames more clearly, his voice rose in panic. "What if the whole forest burns?"

"We just have to keep ahead of the fire." Ben spoke as calmly as he could. He supported Elliot and pulled him forward.

They climbed over tangled vines and fallen logs, traveling slowly but steadily—toward where, or what, they had no idea. The smoke made both of them cough and burned their eyes. The puppy whimpered.

They heard the distant sound of sirens. "It's the fire engines from Carville!" Ben said.

Elliot asked, "They'll put it out right away, won't they?"

Ben knew it could take a while to control a wildfire. "They'll sure try."

From the sound of the engines and the look of the flames, he figured the fire was less than three

miles away, and the park was about three miles from where he lived. So he and Elliot must have traveled roughly parallel to the road. Ben realized they could actually be at some point near his home by now.

The thought filled him with a surge of strength. He remembered they had circled again and again, so he didn't know whether the bungalow would be to the right or the left of them, or how far into the woods they were. Or how to get out.

But at least he had hope now.

Elliot seemed to feel the same way. He put out more effort, using his bad leg as much as he could. Although they didn't know which way to go, they were at least getting farther from the fire. It seemed better than just standing still.

Ben strained his eyes, trying to see a familiar tree or other landmark through the darkness.

But he couldn't make out anything recognizable.

The sirens stopped. The boys told each other the firefighters were working now.

This thought cheered them for a while. They

coughed and battled on, through tangled vines and piercing spiny plants and dried-up ferns.

But as time went by, the boys' spirits sagged. The forest was very quiet, a lonely unknown vastness. Animals seemed to have gone to some distant secret place. No birds sang.

The boys were lost. Lost.

# 8

"Somebody must be looking for us by now," Elliot said. His voice trembled.

"Yes."

"They won't know where to look, though."

"The other kids probably told them we ran into the woods."

"Great," Elliot said. "Even I know that much."

Ben realized it wasn't much of a lead. But it was something.

They struggled on. They didn't know what else to do. Ben was afraid that if they struck out to the right or the left, they might stray farther from the road.

The unending quiet, the choking smoke, the loneliness, ate at his confidence. Elliot seemed a heavy burden now. Even the puppy seemed heavy. Ben coughed and tried to take in a full breath. The air was painfully thick with smoke.

He remembered the moment at the picnic when he had agreed to set off the rockets. It seemed a long time ago. He could hardly believe he had been so stupid, and for what? To do something exciting? To impress Elliot? And now here they were, just trying to survive.

Ben thought if only he could live that moment over again, he would be content to be his own ordinary self, a backwoods boy in Bending Creek, eating Goomby's honey cake and listening to "The Stars and Stripes Forever."

Hope ebbed from him. Dragging Elliot, he took a few more steps, then a few more.

He thought he heard something, a faint familiar wave of sounds.

He stood still, listening, wondering if he had imagined it.

He took a few more steps, a little to the right this time. Again the soft familiar clamor came through the trees, louder.

"What's that?" Elliot asked.

Suddenly Ben knew. He could scarcely get the words out. "It's the bells!"

With a rush of joy, he recognized each one. There was Mr. Hendrick's brass bell, and Miss Alice's I've-got-news bell, and more that belonged to the Olsens and other neighbors. And loudest of all, Goomby's come-home bell, clanging over and over, the best noise Ben had ever heard in his life.

"This way!" Pulling Elliot, Ben veered toward the wonderful discordant sounds.

"I hear them!" Elliot exclaimed.

Both boys laughed, jubilant, exhausted.

They kept following the bells.

Finally they saw the lighted porch of Ben's bungalow through the trees. It was like a glorious ending to a nightmare.

Ben looked up the road. There was no glow in the sky now, no flames. Only smoke, the lingering ghost of a dead fire.

They were safe.

The porch was packed with neighbors, along with Grandpa and Grandma, and Goomby in the middle of them, shaking her big noisy bell for all she was worth.

Both boys whooped with relief. "Here we are!" Ben yelled. "Here we are!"

With their pale smudged faces and torn dirty clothes, the boys stumbled up onto the porch.

"We got him," Ben said proudly, showing the dog.

"Oh, good," Goomby said. The rest of Ben's family and the neighbors huddled around them.

Grandma explained that Lucy Johnson and the other kids had told the boys' families they were in the woods, so Grandpa and Mr. Lorton and some other men had searched for them until the firefighters came and ordered everyone out of the forest.

"We knew we had to find you somehow. The bells seemed like the best way," Goomby said.

Grandpa told Elliot, "We promised your folks we'd call them if you came here, and they promised the same. They've been waiting at home." He added to Ben, "We heard about the rockets." His eyes flashed with anger. "You could have burned down the whole forest."

"And destroyed all of our homes," Mr. Hendrick put in.

"Besides, you worried us nearly to death," Grandma scolded.

"It was that darned dog!" Elliot protested. "If he hadn't taken off like that—"

Miss Alice frowned at him. "I told you to buy a collar and leash."

Grandpa told Elliot, "I'll call your folks." He went inside. Everybody followed him, crowding into the bungalow.

Ben stood apart from the others, hugging the puppy against his chest. He knew he would have to give him to Elliot soon, but he wanted to hold him a little longer.

When the Lortons came, there were more explanations, more scoldings, more anger and joy.

"Well, we'll get on home," Mr. Lorton said finally. "Take your puppy, Elliot."

"I don't want the dog anymore," Elliot said. He turned his weary face to Miss Alice. "You were right—it's a big responsibility. Too big for me."

Ben stared at him. Did he really mean it?

"You're sure?" Mrs. Lorton asked her son.

"I'm *positive*," Elliot said.

"Then I guess—I guess you'll have to give him back to Miss Alice," his mother said. "I'm sorry, Miss Alice. I hope you can find another home for him."

She answered helplessly, "Oh, dear."

*"No,"* Elliot said. "I want to give him to Ben. He cares more about him than I do. He'll watch out for him better." Elliot added, "He already has."

Ben's feelings seemed to form a lump in his throat, choking him.

Goomby glanced at the boys. She said firmly,

"*We'd* like to have a dog." Practical as ever, she added, "They catch rats."

Grandma and Grandpa offered brightly, "Well, that's true. They do."

"So if it's agreeable to Miss Alice, we'll take him," Goomby said.

Miss Alice sighed and smiled. "I'm very relieved. Of course it's agreeable."

The grownups murmured goodbyes. Elliot left with his parents. At the doorway he turned, gave Ben a grin, and joked, "We must take a walk in the woods again sometime."

Ben smiled and returned the joke. "Okay, but not anytime soon."

Soon everybody was gone except the family.

Grandpa and Goomby consulted privately for a minute. Then Grandpa said to Ben, "This is a very serious thing you did. You understand that?"

"Yes, sir."

"The police chief and the chief of the Carville fire department want to talk to you. I'll come home early from work to take you to see them."

"Yes, sir."

"Then for a week you're not to play with the dog or take him out or feed him. Goomby and I will do that, starting tomorrow."

"Okay."

Goomby said firmly, "That's for tomorrow. This is tonight, and Ben's home again."

Grandpa nodded.

Ben went out to the porch with the puppy. Goomby turned off the light and left them alone.

Ben felt guilty and ashamed, and he knew he deserved to feel like that. But after some quiet time, the bad events of the day seemed to slip away. He sat in the porch chair, brimming with happiness.

He patted the sleepy puppy in his lap. His thoughts spun into the future . . . their walks together, the Frisbee games.

He said aloud, "You belong with us. You're our dog."

The pup wagged his tail. Ben knew he didn't really understand—but in a way, maybe he did.